The Push

A Story of Friendship

Written by **PATRICK GRAY**

Illustrated by **JUSTIN SKEESUCK** and **MATT WARESAK**

Tyndale House Publishers, I
Carol Stream, IL

Fountaindale Public Library
Bolingbrook, IL
(630) 759-2102

For our amazing wives, Donna Gray and Kirstin Skeesuck—
thank you for believing in us and tolerating all the crazy we bring to your worlds!

For our children—
never stop loving the world; it is the only thing that can save it.

For our families—
thank you for having faith in us.

For our friends—
we wouldn't be here without you.

We love you all!

Visit Tyndale's website for kids at www.tyndale.com/kids.

TYNDALE is a registered trademark of Tyndale House Publishers, Inc. The Tyndale Kids logo is a trademark of Tyndale House Publishers, Inc.

The Push

Copyright © 2018 by Justin Skeesuck and Patrick Gray. All rights reserved.

Line art by Matt Waresak. Watercolor by Justin Skeesuck. Illustrations copyright © Justin Skeesuck and Patrick Gray.

Back cover photograph of Justin working copyright © Push, Inc. All rights reserved.

Author photographs of Patrick Gray and Justin Skeesuck by Timothy Bryant, copyright © 2016. All rights reserved.

Published in association with The Christopher Ferebee Agency, www.christopherferebee.com.

Scripture taken from the Holy Bible, *New International Version,*® *NIV.*® Copyright © 1973, 1978, 1984, 2011 by Biblica, Inc.® Used by permission. All rights reserved worldwide.

For manufacturing information regarding this product, please call 1-800-323-9400.

For information about special discounts for bulk purchases, please contact Tyndale House Publishers at csresponse@tyndale.com, or call 1-800-323-9400.

ISBN 978-1-4964-2880-6

Printed in the United States of America

24	23	22	21	20	19	18
8	7	6	5	4	3	2

In an ordinary town,
in an ordinary house,
there lived a boy named John.

John slept in a bed like everyone else;
he ate food like everyone else;
he loved to play like everyone else.

But he was different from the other kids in town.

When John was born, his arms and legs didn't work. He couldn't do all the things his friends could do.

He couldn't dress himself.

He couldn't brush his teeth.

He couldn't tie his shoes.

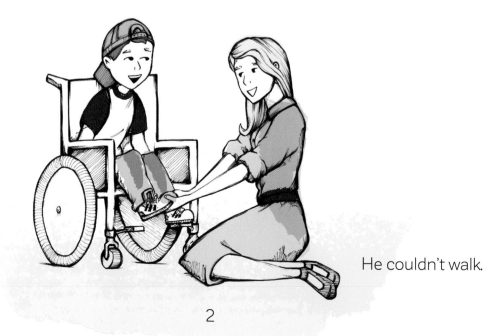

He couldn't walk.

When he wasn't sleeping, he was usually in his wheelchair.

But there were some things John was an expert at.

He could give any statistic about the Boston Red Sox since they got their nickname in 1908.

He could make people laugh until milk came squirting out their noses.

And he could solve the most complicated math problems in his head.

One summer, just before school started, John saw a moving truck at the house next door.

"Would you please wheel me outside so I can see the new neighbors?" John asked his mom.

As his mom parked him at the end of the driveway, John saw a boy carrying a box. He was wearing a Red Sox hat.

"2004!" John shouted.

The boy turned around. "Sixth World Series title!"

"And eleventh American League Pennant!" John replied.

The boy walked over to John. "My name's Marcus."

When Marcus stuck out his hand, John said with a smile, "My hands don't work."

"That's okay," Marcus said, lifting John's hand. "How about this?"

"That will be our handshake!" John said.

In no time, Marcus and John were best friends.

They were in the same class at school. When John wasn't helping Marcus with his math homework, they watched baseball games together or played chess. (Marcus moved John's pieces for him, but John almost always won.) Sometimes they explored the neighborhood, with Marcus skateboarding behind John's wheelchair.

One day at recess, when the leaves were starting to crunch under John's wheelchair, their classmate Timothy handed out invitations to all the boys in the class.

Marcus opened the envelope for John so he could read it.

"We should go!" Marcus said.

"I'm not sure." John looked down. "I can't feed myself."

Marcus shook John's hand just like the first day they met. "If you don't go, who will make us all laugh until our sides hurt? Besides—I can feed you."

You're invited to my birthday party on Friday. Come to my house at 6:00 for pizza, cake, and ice cream!

The day of the party, when everyone was sitting down to eat, John said, "Hey, want to hear a pizza joke?"

"Yeah!" everyone shouted.

"Ah, never mind," John said. "It's too cheesy."

Everybody laughed, and then Marcus held up a piece of pizza for John so he could take a bite.

Every time John needed help eating, Marcus would feed him.

One morning, a few days after winter break, John woke up and looked out his window. The hills around the town were covered with a fresh blanket of white. "No school today!"

Within minutes there was a knock on the door. John heard a familiar voice down the hall.

"Want to play in the snow?" Marcus asked.

"Yeah! Let's go sledding on the hill by the school! But it will be a while before my mom can get me ready."

"That's okay," Marcus said. "I'll do it."

"Great!" John nodded at the closet. "My coat is the green one."

"Got it."

"Gloves?"

"Check."

"Boots?"

"Check."

"Hat?"

"Check."

"Okay, I think we're ready!" John said.

"Hey, do you know what snowmen eat for breakfast?" John asked as Marcus helped him into his wheelchair.

"Uh, I have no idea. Tell me."

"Frosted Flakes!"

Marcus was grinning as they left the house.

The trek to the hill was slow but worth it. They spent the day zipping down on Marcus's sled and trudging up again until patches of grass dotted the white hill.

Back at John's house, Marcus built a snowman in the front yard.

"What did one snowman say to the other snowman?" John asked.

Marcus smiled and shook his head. "Tell me."

John took a long sniff. "Do you smell carrots?"

Marcus erupted in laughter. "That's your best one yet!"

"This is the best snow day yet," John said.

Whenever John wanted to play in the snow, Marcus would dress him.

One warm Saturday, the neighbor kids were outside playing baseball in the park. John kept the stats. When they took a break between innings, Ben announced, "Hey, we just got a new TV! Mom says we can have a movie night at my house."

The boys buzzed with excitement. Ben had the best movie-watching room in town, complete with beanbag chairs and a popcorn machine.

John looked at Marcus. "Are you going?"

"Only if you go."

"But they have all those stairs," John said.

"I'll carry you!" Marcus said.

That night, all the neighborhood boys gathered at Ben's house, including John. They watched the movie, ate popcorn, and talked about the lineup of Red Sox pitchers for the season.

Whenever Ben had a movie night, John would go, and Marcus would carry him.

At the end of the school year, the class planned a field trip to explore the hills behind the school.

They were going to look at the trees, search for animals, and hike the trails. They'd finish the day by roasting marshmallows over a fire while they watched the sun set on the horizon.

John looked at Marcus. "I really want to go!"

Marcus smiled and said, "I'll push you!"

The day of the hike, a light rain was falling. The ground squished under Marcus's feet, and the wheels of John's wheelchair kept getting stuck in the mud.

As Marcus cleared sticks and rocks from the path, a smile spread across John's face. "How can you tell that a tree is a dogwood?"

"I have no clue," Marcus said.

"By its bark!"

As they trudged beside a stream, the ground got even soggier. "You should keep going without me," John said. "Then you can keep up with the rest of the group."

"Nah. We may be slow, but we're having more fun than everyone else."

Several years later, the two boys hiked up the same hill, behind the same school. They sat in the same spot and roasted marshmallows again, watching the same sun set behind the same horizon.

Marcus put a marshmallow on his stick and inched it toward the fire. "Want one?" he asked.

John nodded, but his mind was somewhere else. "Hey, Marcus. Why are you friends with me? I'm so different from everyone else."

Marcus shot him a sideways grin. "Yeah, I guess you're different. There's no one who can make me laugh like you do or who has taught me more about math. There's no one I'd rather watch baseball with or eat pizza with or play in the snow with or hike through the woods with. Should I keep going?"

"I never thought about it that way," John said. "But what about all the things I can't do?"

Marcus shrugged. "I guess there are some things you can't do. But that goes for me, too. I can barely draw a stick figure. I can't remember the punch lines to jokes. The only reason I passed math is because of your help. And I can't name half the roster for the Red Sox this year."

"That's not what I'm talking about," John said.

"What do you mean?" Marcus asked.

John turned to Marcus, and with a tear in his eye, he said,

"When I couldn't feed myself, you fed me.

"When I needed help getting ready, you dressed me.

"When I wanted to watch a movie with our friends but couldn't get down the steps, you carried me.

"And when I wanted to explore the hills with the rest of the class, you pushed me. You've been my hands and my feet for most of my life. I wish I could do that for you.

A smile spread across Marcus's face. "You have done something even greater for me."

"How?" John shot him a confused look.

"When I fed you, you taught me how to take my time, how to be patient," Marcus said. "When I dressed you, you showed me how I can help other people. When I carried you, you made me stronger so I could keep carrying you as we got older. And when I pushed you, you showed me how much joy there is in giving everything for someone else. I may have fed you, dressed you, carried you, and pushed you. But you have shown me how to laugh and how to live."

Marcus took a bite of his gooey marshmallow. "That's why we're friends, right? We're stronger together than we are on our own."

"Yeah, but sometimes I wish we could switch places. I wish I could push you instead."

"You do! Every single day." Marcus paused. "I push you in your wheelchair, but you push me to be a better person."

Marcus shook John's hand, just the way he had on the first day they met. And they ate another marshmallow.

Spread love everywhere you go.
Let no one ever come to you without leaving happier.

MOTHER TERESA

Be devoted to one another in love. Honor one another above yourselves.

ROMANS 12:10

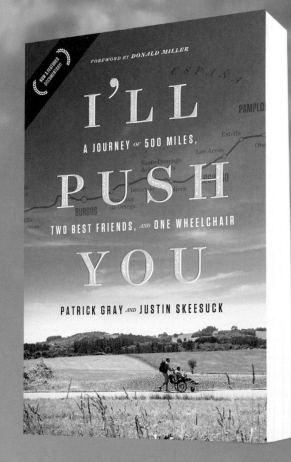

TWO BEST FRIENDS, 500 MILES, ONE WHEELCHAIR, AND THE CHALLENGE OF A LIFETIME.